By the same author and illustrator team:

All the Things Santa Claus Will Never Do
ISBN 978-0-7643-6217-0
All the Things a Teacher Will Never Say
ISBN 978-0-7643-6218-7
All the Things Mom Will Never Say
ISBN 978-0-7643-6331-3

 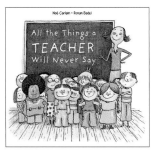 

Copyright © 2022 by Schiffer Publishing, Ltd.

Translated from the French by Simulingua, Inc.

Originally published as *Tout ce qu'un Papa dira toujours* by L'Elan Vert, Saint-Pierre-des-Corps © 2015

Library of Congress Control Number: 2021942847

Type set in GEDProvidence/Infant

ISBN: 978-0-7643-6330-6
Printed in India

Published by Schiffer Kids
An imprint of Schiffer Publishing, Ltd.
4880 Lower Valley Road
Atglen, PA 19310
Phone: (610) 593-1777; Fax: (610) 593-2002
Email: Info@schifferbooks.com
Web: www.schifferbooks.com

For our complete selection of fine books on this and related subjects, please visit our website at www.schifferbooks.com. You may also write for a free catalog.

Schiffer Publishing's titles are available at special discounts for bulk purchases for sales promotions or premiums. Special editions, including personalized covers, corporate imprints, and excerpts, can be created in large quantities for special needs. For more information, contact the publisher.

All the Things DAD will Always SAY

Noé Carlain

Ronan Badel

Schiffer **Kids**™

4880 Lower Valley Road, Atglen, PA 19310

My sweet dad
says the same things
over and over again.
They say all daddies are like that.
Mine, well, what he will always say
is . . .

"When I was your age,
I used to spend hours doing my homework every night."

Dad and his friends,
the night before their big math test.

"I have everything under control ..."

"You need to practice
and work hard at it every day."

"Don't be afraid!
A little critter like that can't hurt you."

But apparently
it depends on the little critter ...

Dad always says:
"Patience is a virtue! Good things come to those who wait."

Except in traffic jams ten minutes before the opening pitch of the baseball game.

"Now where did that remote go?"

"Honestly, I am the
only organized person
in this house!"

"Bon appétit, my little one!"

"Above all, remember—style and grace."

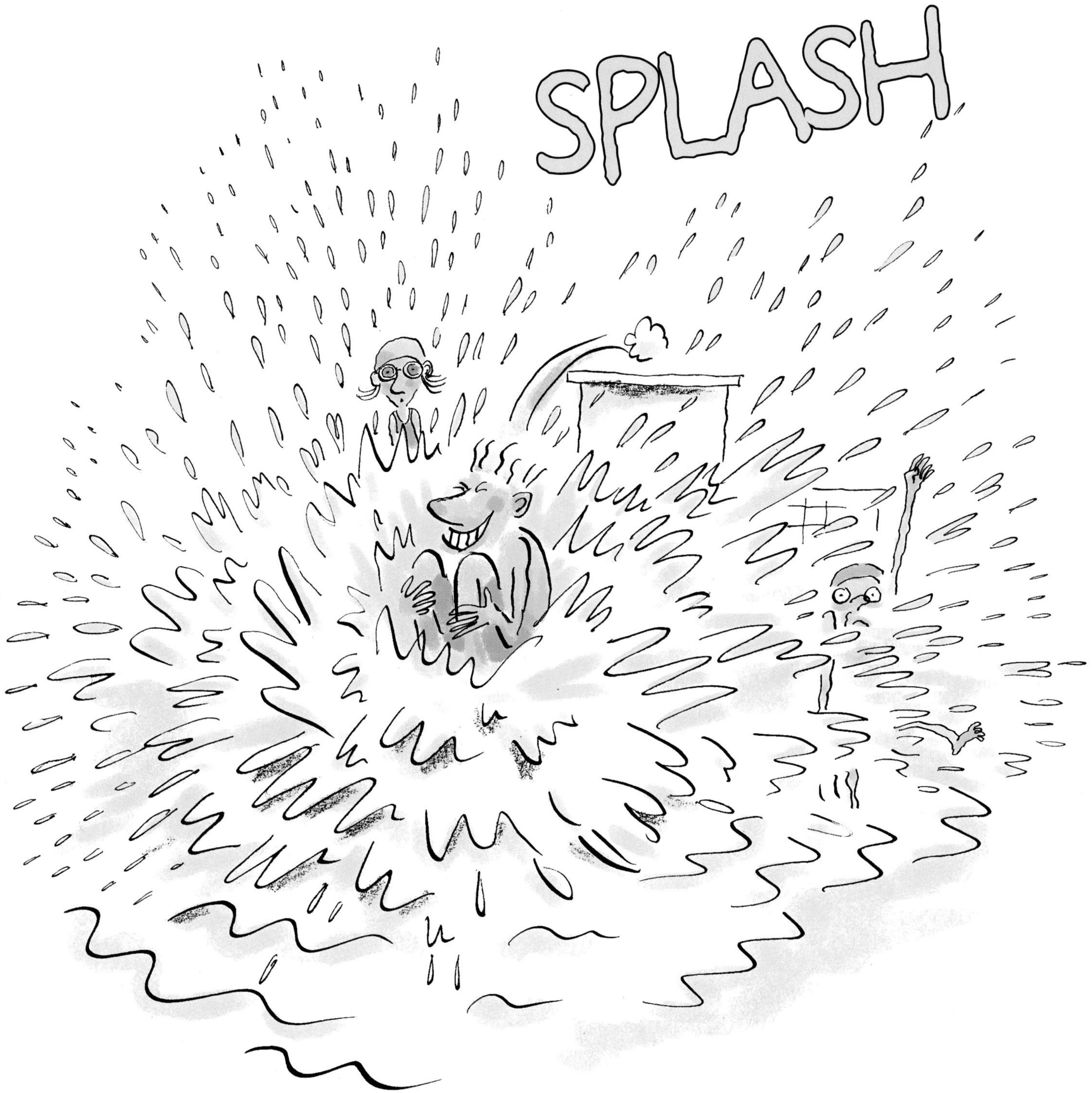
SPLASH

"When I was your age, I read only the best books by the greatest authors."

But ... sometimes he stays in the bathroom a long, long time reading gossip magazines.

"You see, kiddo, dad knows all about car repairs.
We'll be on the road again in five minutes."

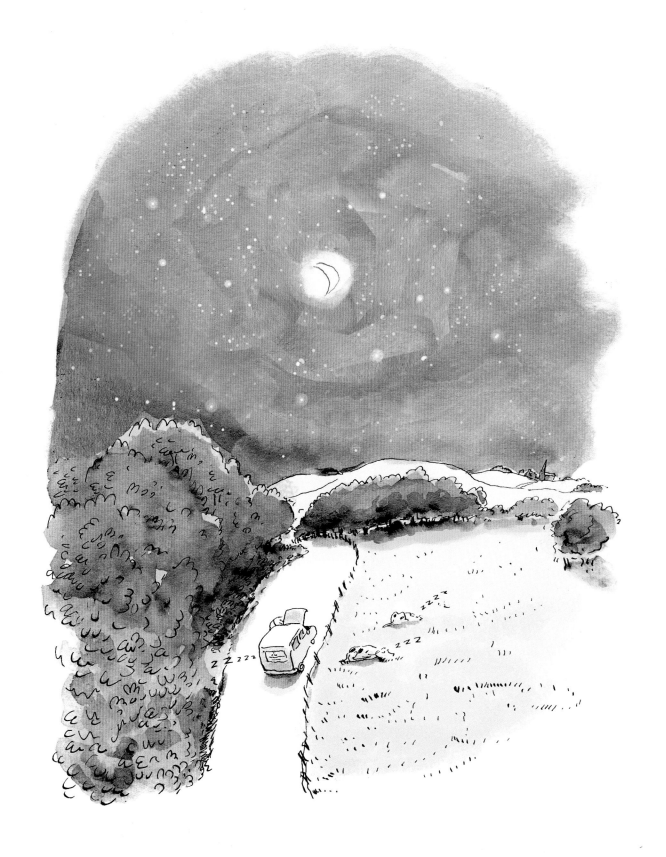

But what Dad always says,
and what I love so much, is ...

"Climb up on my shoulders, my little one.
Come and see how much bigger
the world is when we are together!"